I0672128

I Have Touched the Other Side

Based on A true story

Sue Riester

I Have Touched the Other Side

Based on a True Story

By Sue Riester

Published by Maravilla Publishing

http://www.maravillapublishing.com

Cover design by Sue Riester and Aaron Stramaglia

ISBN 978-0-9552409-2-8

This book is dedicated to:

The Power of the Earth that is waiting to be rediscovered.

Chapter 1

In this world of magic and illusion, vision is often something that cannot be depended upon. Things are not always as they seem. If one opens their mind to new possibilities, vision becomes a different thing entirely. Everything takes on a new meaning, and what is truth, reveals itself in unusual ways.

In the eighteenth century, there were small towns dotting the Italian countryside. Large cities were not large by modern standards. The small villages had their own politics, their own ways. There were some open communications between towns, but for the most part there was a sense of isolation, and the towns were kingdoms in their own right.

In one particular town, the politics were that of evil. The town was controlled by a man who would do anything to grow in status. He was able to do whatever he wanted whenever he wanted. There was no limit to his greed. He hungered for power and money. That hunger went deep, and could not be satiated. He wanted to own every business in town. If he desired something, he could not be stopped. He would enjoy stopping in to visit people in town. Not because he longed for friendship, but because he loved the way people would squirm around him. He knew that no one felt comfortable with him. Throughout his life, he learned to enjoy the discomfort that others felt around him. And he would always make them pay for that. It was the core of his hunger. He found strength in this darkness. The feeling of loathing others felt for him, was something he could hold on to and understand.

Roberto had just finished dealings for his fourth business in town. He could relax in the thoughts of his accomplishments. It was a wonderful feeling for him to make that man grovel for his life. And he knew he was making a mark for himself in this town. He heard the whisperings, and was glad of it. He knew the townsfolk were referring to him as the devil. He felt in many ways, the title was deserved. After all, did he not just take over the millinery with little cost to himself? The power seemed to flow through his veins. Now, where could he direct his attention next?

As time went by and Roberto was relishing his role in the town politics, he developed a desire to obtain the town bakery. The bakery would make a nice addition to his collection. Now the question remained; how to go about it. How could he derive the most pleasure from achieving his desire? There was always such an empty hole in his heart that needed filling, even upon completion of his latest project.

So, the planning began. He would take over the bakery. Roberto knew that Santi would not want to sell. He and his wife had run the business for the past twenty years. The business had been in the family for generations, and they had planned to pass it on to their children. He would want to keep the family recipes and the knowledge gleaned from all the years Santi's family had owned the business. A plan formed quickly, and Roberto was prepared to execute his plan ruthlessly.

Roberto stopped in to see Santi. Roberto's very presence sent a chill down Santi's spine. He knew Roberto was an evil man, and so he expected the worse. As usual when Roberto was concerned the worst did happen. Roberto started the discussion of purchasing the bakery. Santi of course refused. Roberto spent the next moments in silence. Then he told Santi that it didn't matter what he wanted to do. He intended to purchase the bakery, and nothing that Santi would decide could change that. There was to be no debate on the subject. Roberto would own the bakery.

"Santi you know if I want your business, it is mine."

"I will not give up my family business. This is the lifeblood of my family. It has been in the family for generations, and that is where it will stay."

"I don't think so. It would be easier on you, if you would just turn the bakery over to me now."

"You know I can't allow that."

"Then you will pay the price, and it will be a heavy one."

Santi talked with his friends in town. The feedback was just what Santi expected.

"Santi, I saw the devil was in your house."

"Yes, he wants my business, my bakery."

"You know he will find a way to get what he wants."

"Yes, but I must resist. He can't always have it his way."

"Be careful Santi. Watch him carefully, he plans, and no one has yet found a way to stop him. Be careful."

And so it went as Santi spoke with his friends in town. They warned him. But it stuck in Santi's craw that he should give his family's business up without a fight. He knew it was crazy, but also irresistible. If the town worked together, perhaps they could send Roberto on his way. Perhaps they could help him save his family's business. When it was their turn, they would feel the same as Santi. If only he could convince them that his was a worthy fight. And so, Santi spoke with his friends and neighbors trying to convince them to help. But, this was to no avail. No one would stand up to this force of evil; they had given up their power before the challenge was ever made.

Roberto was in the mood for talking as well. He went to everyone that Santi had spoken to, and told the townsfolk to stay out of the matter. Roberto threatened the people in town, making it clear that their interference would be unwelcome and dealt with harshly.

The people of the town liked Santi, but they held a fear of Roberto. No one liked it when the devil entered their house. Santi was like them, and they felt sorry for him, that he had attracted the attention of such a man as Roberto. However, they liked living themselves, and no friendship could make them put their lives at risk. Their families were important to them as well.

So, Santi, do what he will, could not fight this man. One day Roberto came to visit Santi, and then Santi breathed his last breath. The bakery went to Roberto, leaving Santi's family without.

Santi's wife Helen was sick with grief over her husband's death. She wailed for justice, but there was none. Everyone was too fearful of Roberto. He was so mean. He was evil. They knew he would have everything his way. They believed in the illusion of his strength, and thus made him stronger by their belief.

But, Helen could not let go of her fear and hatred for this man. He had taken everything from her. Helen was forced to work for

Roberto, if she wanted to feed her children. It was the only way she knew to make money. And so, she continued to bake. She made the bread and pastries that her friends and neighbors had become accustomed to. Her fear and hatred grew. Every time she saw Roberto, and that was at least once a day, he seemed to gloat over his accomplishments. She had no opportunities for forgiveness, he wouldn't leave her be. He wouldn't let her heal. There was no one for her to turn to, and so her hatred for Roberto and the circumstances of her life grew.

Roberto got away with murder. This made him laugh. He knew now that he could have his way with the people of this town. They were too weak to fight any of his advances. It made no difference that they referred to him as the devil. It was better that way. It made what he intended to do much easier. They would all just give him what he wanted. His bold plan had paid off in ways he could not have imagined at the inception of the plan.

Roberto continued to tighten his grip on the town. He continued to manipulate the people. He continued his visits to his fellow villagers. How he enjoyed causing them pain, both physical and mental. Then one day he thought it might be worth a trip to a neighboring village. See what might be available outside the little world he had built. Surely if he was successful here on his test grounds, there would be further success for him down the road.

He packed his things for a week in the neighboring village. He got in his carriage, and took off down the road.

People were glad to see him go, though they knew not to say anything about it. He would be back. This they knew. The fear grew on them as they realized how this evil was growing. He was trying to expand to other areas of the countryside. Perhaps there would be nowhere for any of them to go soon. There was no law, no justice to stop him from his ways. Roberto looked bent on taking the world, one piece at a time.

Time went by, and Roberto did not return as expected. It was silly really; it was not as if they ever wanted to see him again. And then one day someone came in from the neighboring town. With him the neighbor brought Roberto. Roberto had met his end. The carriage wheel had broken. The forward momentum had caused Roberto to lurch forward suddenly on to the brake handle. He was speared through the gut, and his body ceased to exist.

Roberto, as he left his body, raged with anger. How could this happen. He was on the verge of building his own little empire. And here it was all snatched from him. His carriage wheel had broken, and surprised him with his death. No, this couldn't be happening! There had to be a way to reclaim what was his, there had to be a way. And then it came to him, a way that he could endure, keeping memory of his thoughts and desires. A way of keeping his loathing of others, and the joy he found in making them suffer. It was perfect really. Now he could exact a greater vengeance on Santi, for trying to deny him his desires. Yes, they would all continue to pay dearly for every imagined slight. The way was clear, and the path of hatred had presented the way. Yes, no matter if he might find himself trapped in the illusion of time. It was worth the price. How bad could it be?

Chapter 2

The war was over, the latest war to end all wars. Men and women started to return to their homes. It was a time to rebuild lives and families. Families that had not had a chance to begin were started. Families that had begun could now be complete. People had been through a horrible time, and were now ready to cherish every day, every moment.

And so it was with Rosa and Francisco. They had started a family before the war, and in there joy of being reunited, they found that they had not quite completed the numbers in their family.

Rosa had been very sick through this pregnancy, and was anxious to deliver this child. Her other two children had been much easier to carry. She had experienced just a little morning sickness in the first few weeks, and then relatively easy deliveries.

The plan was the same for this pregnancy as for the last two; Rosa would deliver at home, a common practice at the time. It was all arranged, she was seeing the doctor regularly now that she was in her eighth month of pregnancy.

The time finally came, Rosa was in labor. When Frank called for the doctor, he found the doctor was suddenly unavailable. He couldn't reach him or anyone. It didn't matter that this was his third time, Frank was nervous, this time felt different to him. So he frantically started calling numbers for doctors in the phone book. How could it be that no one was able to come to deliver this baby? Frank felt like he had entered a dreamscape that had no ending. He prayed and pleaded with God, and went back to the phone book. Finally he got an answer, finally his prayers were answered, and someone would come and help.

Dr. Scott showed up at the door like an angel of mercy. He went right back to see Rosa. She was almost ready to go for the final push. This being her third child, events progressed quickly. She finally delivered just after midnight.

Frank waited outside the room, he knew he would get in the way, and quite honestly did not want to faint. The doctor called to Frank and asked him to come in the room. Rosa was there, wide awake, and the strain gone from her face. Her expression was replaced with sadness. Frank stood there with his jaw to the floor. What was happening?

Dr. Scott said "I'm sorry the baby was strangled by his own chord during delivery."

Frank started begging, surely there was something they could do, something they could try.

Dr. Scott explained that he could try some techniques that might revive the baby, but that even if he did survive, his son might never be normal, surely he would be mentally retarded.

Frank took one look at Rosa and then turned to Dr. Scott. "Please he begged, please try."

So, Dr. Scott tried, he worked on the baby tirelessly. He lost track of the time, but kept at it. Miraculously the baby took a breath, and then another. He would live. At least for the moment it appeared he would survive. But, was survival enough? Surely he had saved a baby who would have to live out his days without the benefit of a brain.

Dr. Scott pulled out his pocket watch and checked the time. It had been thirty minutes since the baby boy had been born. He turned to Frank and Rosa and said "It's a miracle that your son is alive, pray that he grows strong and mentally well."

Dr. Scott walked out the door, and no matter how Frank and Rosa searched, they were never able to find him again. More than that, no one had ever heard of this mystery doctor. He had simply walked into their lives, and left them with both a miracle and questions about the destiny of this child.

So they did what they could. They took care of their son, and they prayed for him.

Chapter 3

Vincent was a healthy boy, well liked and smarter than most of his friends. He played his intelligence down; he didn't want to seem better than the rest of his friends. He enjoyed being outside playing, inventing new games and new ways of having fun. Nevertheless, he did well at school, and his friends did not begrudge him anything. He did well, but did not brag or make a big deal over his accomplishments. This made it very easy to like Vince, and he had no shortage of friends.

Vincent lived in a smaller town in eastern Pennsylvania. He had an older brother and sister, and loving parents. His home was typical for the area in which he lived; it was a 2 story, 3 bedroom house. It was built in the early nineteenth century, and must have had one hundred coats of paint on it by now. His father kept the house and yard under good repair. At an early age his father had taught him how to mow lawn, weed garden and other basic outdoor tasks.

He always told Vincent that these were good things to know, and he would need to know these skills someday when he had a family of his own. Vincent was never sure how to take this, as he was too young to even consider that he might one day have his own family. But, he was a good child, and did what was asked of him, sometimes lighter of heart than at other times.

Vince got along well enough with his brother, Richard who was five years older than Vincent. Richard looked out for Vincent. However, it wasn't really that necessary.

His sister Carol was seven years older than Vincent. They had little in common, and would talk to pass time between them, but they were really of two different worlds. After all, she was a girl and so much older. She was kind to Vincent, but spent little time with him.

When Vincent would get ready for bed, he would talk with his mother asking various questions about his younger years. At seven, the long history of his years was interesting to him. Stories of himself as a baby or child were like bedtime stories. After all, his own adventures as remembered by his mother embellished or not, were fascinating.

He especially enjoyed the story of his birth. His mother would go over the details of his birth. She created the proper drama when telling his story. He would drift off to sleep wondering about himself. His own existence was a mystery to him. As he grew older the mystery deepened. He understood more about life itself, and was amazed that he should be alive. The thought of this mystery would often send him into great introspection. Was there a purpose to life? Was there a purpose to his life specifically? It seemed to him that there must be a special reason for his existence, especially when one considered the extraordinary circumstances surrounding his birth. When no clear answers came, he would fall asleep, leaving room for the story to be retold by his mother, and allowing him to repeat his self absorptive thoughts.

Vincent had many opportunities to spend time with his extended family. His grandparents from both his mothers and fathers side of the family, his aunts and uncles. His father came from a family of four brothers. His mother was an only child. His mothers' parents were kind and doting. When they had responsibility for Vincent, they would keep a close eye on him. He wasn't used to this but in his younger years he had to be accepting.

Time spent with his fathers' parents was a whole different story. His grandfather, Joseph, was a nice enough man, and he enjoyed being with him. Vincent's grandfather had plenty of experience with boys, and was able to tell him stories of his own youth. In times when technology was essentially non-existent, it took imagination to amuse oneself. His grandfather had always spent his free time climbing trees, looking to the horizon. He was always looking for better circumstances, better times. One of Joseph's favorite things to do as a child was to find a tree of just the right girth. A tree that would hold his weight while climbing it until he just reached the top. Then the tree would gently drop him to the ground. He could repeat this process several times, until the tree became too accustomed to the activity. Then the tree would start bending to the ground with Joseph on it, way before he reached the top of the tree. Vincent's grandfather would walk with him; show him how to find the right type and size of tree. The special time they spent together, would always leave Vincent with fond memories of his grandfather.

Vincent was always very interested in his family and as they walked, his grandfather, would tell him stories. Joseph told stories of his own parents and of their old home far away.

Joseph had said his own mother was a very nasty person. He had always looked for ways to get away from her, and came to America to do just that. He had met his wife Martha here in the United States, and they were happy at first. Then they went back to Italy to visit his father, Giuseppe. He really had no interest in seeing his mother, but she was there just the same. Josephs' visit with his father had been very pleasant. He was able to walk with him alone and talk about the details of their lives during their time apart.

Apparently, Joseph's mother had gotten worse over the years. It was believed that she had a mental condition that caused her behavior. No one was sure exactly what was wrong, but they knew she had not always been this way. She was no longer a person that anyone wanted to spend time around, and in fact most people would actively avoid her.

Unfortunately for Martha, she ended up spending most of their visit with Joseph's mother, Isabella. She did the best with her circumstance. Isabella was old, and very mean. But, for Martha, this was going to be a short visit. Joseph had prepared her for the fact that his mother was not pleasant to be around. She felt she could put up with Isabella's abuse for the short time they would be in Italy to visit. They didn't speak the same language, but Martha felt sure she understood Isabella's intent. Het visage was skewed. Her tone was dark.

As fate would have it, Joseph's mother, Isabella, passed away while he was visiting his father. Joseph and Martha stayed for the funeral.

Martha felt sad for Joseph, she knew that Joseph really didn't care about his mother; she was no longer really his mother. She had become something else to him, but was definitely not the mother he had grown up with, and loved as a child. He had grieved for the loss years before, and did not care to do so again.

When the funeral was over, Joseph and Martha stayed on for awhile with his father Giuseppe. When they finally returned home, a peace had come over Joseph. His mother was at rest, and her struggles with the illness that had changed her so was over. The evil that had become her life was laid to rest.

So, when Vincent watched how his grandmother treated his grandfather, it set him to wonder.

His grandfather had developed severe asthma in his later years. He had required several sets of inhalers. Vincent would watch as his grandmother would hold those inhalers, his grandfather gasping for breath. Martha would stand over him,

"So, Joseph, having trouble breathing?"

"Too bad that you're having so much trouble."

"Bet you'd give anything for a nice clear, fresh breath of air."

"Come on Joseph take a deep breath."

"Can't do it?"

"What's the matter Joseph, you're looking a bit purple?"

"Do you need this inhaler?"

Joseph would nod, his eyes pleading for help. Needing the relief the inhaler would offer. These were the worst scenes to watch. And there was nothing to be done. Grandmother

Martha would continue in this way no matter who would watch. It never mattered if you would try to stop her. She had her own agenda, and would carry through with it until she got what satisfaction she could derive from the dramatic scene.

"Well Joseph, you're not quite ready for it the way I see it."

"I think I'll just wait and see how long it takes for you to pass out."

"Maybe I'll let you die this time. I wonder how long *that* will take."

"Surely you can gasp out just one more breath?"

And when Martha felt sure that Joseph was close to dying, she would give him that breath with the inhaler. The medicine would start to take effect, and he would come back to life.

"See Joseph, you better be good to me, I have the inhaler. I decide if you live or die. I decide how much you will suffer either way."

And Joseph did suffer, in more ways than this, His lovely Martha was lost forever, and it was all his fault, he was sure of it. His mother's illness seemed to pass on to his Martha. Obviously whatever this sickness was, he was immune, but not his Martha. He wished he had never taken her to Italy. It was his fault. And in his own way he felt he deserved to suffer. After so many years, he wasn't sure he even wanted to live. So, if Martha would concede to give him the inhaler, or not, it didn't matter. He had caused her suffering, now she would cause his. They were locked together in a struggle that seemingly had no end.

Then one time as the drama was playing out, Martha was too late with the inhaler. Joseph's struggle with his asthma had ended. His struggle with his mother's and Martha's disease had ended.

Chapter 4

Vincent grew older, his parents had moved to New Jersey, and he saw little of his grandmother. That suited him just fine. It was always his grandfather he had enjoyed visiting.

He graduated from high school and it was time to go to college. College would take him back to eastern Pennsylvania.

Vince's grandmother lived in a rather large home. The third floor was more of a finished attic. It would due as a small apartment, and give Vince some of the privacy he craved.

It would have been totally unacceptable to live in the house with his grandmother. As it was, he could manage living in the small third floor apartment above his grandmother.

The apartment was hot in the summer and cold in the winter. It was not well insulated, and the temperature of the apartment rose and fell according to the weather outside. He had small space heaters for the winter. In the summer he used a small air conditioner for his bedroom. He was able to go home and visit with his parents often, so the situation was tolerable.

Vince had two loves at this time; Science and Music. He spent a great deal of time studying and became adept in chemistry. During his free time he taught himself to play the guitar. In keeping with the times, he played and sang at his friends parties. He played guitar with several of his friends. In fact in those days there were plenty of opportunities to play in the local bars. He wasn't good enough to become famous, but he was good enough to eventually meet the woman he would marry. In the mean time he loved his music and could get lost in the melodies he played on his guitar.

While living at his grandmother's home, he did have the opportunity to spend time with her. Being a man of science, he was curious about his grandmother. He wasn't exactly sure how to bring it up to her. The consequences of a misplaced question could be dire.

One day Vince was helping his grandmother move some furniture around. She offered him a sandwich in payment. Her mood was fairly light, and she was telling Vince a story that happened in the supermarket. Someone had left a cart near the checkout counter blocking her way through the aisle. She had taken that cart wheeled it away and waited for the owner to return. When the owner of the shopping cart returned, she reprimanded that person severely. She was cruel and had made that person feel terrible.

Vince turned to her, and said "Martha, you're a mean old bitch aren't you."

She replied "You have no idea."

For some reason this simple statement sent chills down his spine. He was beginning to feel that she was right. He had no idea just how bad she could be. And he had seen her at her worst. She was capable of a great deal of meanness, but now he had the feeling that he had only seen the tip of the proverbial iceberg and her actions were truly evil.

He was afraid, in a way that had never seemed possible.

He continued to live in that house, with his grandmother downstairs from him until he married. He kept more to himself and avoided Martha more diligently.

Martha passed away just two years after Vince married Norma.

Chapter 5

Vince had married. He found a job as a chemist after college. He and Norma were able to find an apartment in eastern Pennsylvania. They lived there until after their first daughter was born. By then they had saved enough to put a down payment on a house in the Pennsylvania Mountains.

Vince loved the area they chose to live in. Hiking was easily available. The scenery out each window was magnificent. Living here he felt full of life and a close contact with nature.

Vince and Norma spent many happy years together. They had children, four girls. All were born healthy, and were comfortable in their family unit.

The girls did all the normal type of activity. Gwen was more into sports, and was involved in all the team sports. There was a great deal of activity in getting her to all her practices and games. There was never a time when you could want for more to do.

Terry was the second born, and was more like her father. She was introspective, and spent a great deal of time thinking about her life. How could she grow? Was she here to help people? What was her path in life? Were there more ways to help people than the obvious? Terry would know things were going to happen before they happened. She could also see things that not everyone could see. She knew it was a gift, but it was a strange gift. Who could she turn to for help in unraveling some of the mysteries she encountered in her day to day life? Some might classify her as an Indigo child.

Terry was lucky, and she knew it. Her father had insight; he had a way of seeing things from a different point of view. She knew he had some similar experiences, and was grateful that he felt comfortable enough to share his thoughts with her. She knew that he didn't easily share his feelings and thoughts with others. In this way, Vince grew very close with Terry, they shared abilities, and they knew there was safety in sharing their experiences with each other. After all, some of their thoughts if spoken openly would have the general public laughing and jeering. Their gift was not easily understood by others. They stayed open and unafraid of their abilities because they could share with each other.

Vince's relationship with Terry was in no way exclusive of his relationship with their other daughters. He loved them equally, and he knew they loved him. His relationship was just different with Terry. Eventually, the others would come to understand their gifts, talk about it. Some of them even had some interesting experiences of their own.

Sandy was Vince's third daughter. She was smart and spent her time studying and reading. She couldn't get enough of the written word. Sandy would often use a flashlight under her covers to continue reading when everyone else was sleeping.

Darlene was Vince's fourth daughter. She was a girly girl. She loved playing dress up as a child, and was a lovely child. She enjoyed individual sports like skiing, these types of sports she could use to measure against herself. It's true that all sports give a person a way to measure themselves, but team sports involved more external show of competition. For her it was more about the competition within herself.

Vince loved his family, and loved spending time with them. He kept his over time to a minimum so that he could spend more time with them. He knew he would never regret that choice. It was often said that near the end of a persons' life, no one ever expressed a regret that they didn't spend more time at work.

He would take his family on hikes, spend time at the beach. Vince also enjoyed taking them all on vacations to see the country. He tried to get them to as many National Parks as he could. These were the areas of our country that were preserved in their pristine condition. The energy in these places was strong in the Earths' true magic. The nature of the energy was that of the old earth, you could feel the difference in these areas that never experienced the full presence of people. In these places people could come in, blend with the energy of the old earth, and come out completely renewed. Vince loved this feeling, and hoped that his wife and daughters could feel it too. He hoped that they would make it all a part of themselves and cherish it.

Spending time with his family, learning more about his wife and daughters were the things that made him truly happy in this time frame. He even started to put aside his thoughts of a higher purpose. For now this was his higher purpose, being with his family, and it was enough.

During the years that he was raising his family, his grandmother, Martha, finally passed away. No one mourned her passing too much. None of Vince's daughters could remember her, as she died when Gwen was very young. For this, Vince was happy. He knew his girls would never have to see what his grandmother was capable of.

Fortunately, he would not have to protect them from her, and could lead his life in a happy, loving way with no outside interference.

Chapter 6

Vince was creating a good life for himself. He had frequent contact with his brother. Richard lived in New Jersey, and did well for himself. He never married, but he did work hard and eventually found himself in a home on the Jersey shore. Vince enjoyed visiting him from time to time, bringing his family with him. It was always nice to take at least one vacation week and spend the time with Richard on the shore.

His sister Carol never married either. Her life took another turn. She lived in New Jersey in an apartment just south of Newark. She was an accountant, not a thrilling job, but she was able to care for herself, and to live a life more involved in culture. She was close to New York City, and was able to go in for plays, shopping and some night life. Her life was coming along very nicely. She had met a wonderful man who also appreciated the arts. She was so hopeful that this might be the one for her to settle down with. She imagined that they would marry, but she could not imagine children being a part of that package.

Carol and Dan were on a little getaway vacation up in the Green Mountains of Vermont, when her grandmother Martha passed away. Richard had called and told her that she needed to come right home, they were planning on burying Martha immediately, there would be no wake.

Carol became very angry at the news. Dan of course was very understanding.

"Carol, it's okay, we can always come back and start in where we left off."

"No Dan, It's not okay, You never knew my grandmother, she was so mean, and now she's taking away my time with you."

Dan didn't understand why Carol was so angry with the situation. What was the big deal, there were only a few days lost. It was also hard to understand Carols' attitude for Martha. The situation was beyond his experience, and he felt that no matter what had transpired, this was still Carol's grandmother, and she should be more upset that she passed, not upset that her death was putting a crimp on her plans.

In fact Carol never got past her anger. Dan noticed that Carol spent a good deal of time being angry. They never got back to Vermont, and Dan extricated himself from the relationship before things got out of hand. Carol just wasn't the same person she used to be. She seldom smiled any more, and lately had started pulling some mean tricks on him. He knew when to cut his losses and got out as quickly as he could. It was over for him.

Dan made the right choice. Carol had developed meanness about her.

Vince thought back on his grandfathers' stories, and was wondering if maybe there wasn't a genetic problem here. It didn't quite track though. Was it environmental? Was there some genetic difficulty that made the women in his family easy prey to some organism? These thoughts nagged at him, but only because he had four daughters, and didn't want to see the degeneration in them that he had learned to see in Martha through his grandfathers' eyes.

Carol continued working in the accounting firm. She was in a position where she was able to do some account manipulation if she desired. She was bonded and her character was vouched for by an independent firm. Carol had been honest in all her dealings until Martha died.

Since Dan left her, an unassailable sorrow had come over her. She felt she would never find true love again. So, she decided to leave the thought of love behind. Money would be better, once you had money, you could count on it being there. It couldn't just decide to walk away from you.

So Carol developed a plan to scam money out of the corporation she worked for. She was successful in removing over a quarter of a million dollars from this company. She was unsure of how long she should keep working the scam. The longer you stayed in these scams, the more comfortable a person would get. At some point the risk would outweigh the benefit of staying where she was. She did not want to get caught. The thought of facing charges was unthinkable. But she had grown accustomed to having the extra money. Life was easier this way, more stressful, but much nicer than it could have been.

As Carol spent time deliberating on what she should do next, she had news that her mother had passed on. She would have to think about this. Her father had a fair amount of money, maybe something could be gleaned from the situation.

Carol left her job in New York. She came home and played the good daughter. She helped clear her fathers' home of her mothers' belongings.

The jewelry was after all, hers. She helped her father with the cooking and cleaning, and took on the role of lady of the house. Vince and Richard were okay with her choice. Really, could they stop her? But, they did notice her change in behavior and thought they should keep a bit of an eye on her activities. This chore fell to Richard more often than Vince based on his proximity. Vince no longer cared about his sister; he knew she had succumbed to the same evil disease that had plagued his family throughout history.

Carol did take care of her father through the years. It was not always pleasant for him, but Carol stayed focused on his money, so she didn't have a great deal of time to spend thinking about his comfort or lack of amenities.

Carol worried only about herself. She took over her fathers' bank accounts. It seemed the logical thing to do. She was an accountant, and he never really spent any time learning how to dispense money. His thoughts had been all about earning money.

Frank had recently retired, and was looking toward a long happy retirement with Rosa. She had died suddenly of a heart attack, and he was broken hearted. Rosa had been everything to him. It was difficult to imagine life without her. Having Carol stay with him twenty years ago, might have been a good proposition to him. However, in recent years, Carol was not the same woman. Sadly she reminded him of his own mother, Martha. She didn't seem to be as nasty as Martha, but she didn't have the years of practice that Martha had. Frank decided that if he had any real issues with Carol, he would let Vince or Richard know. They could help him if the situation started to go bad.

So, Carol stayed with her father. She used her role as her father's helper to slowly slide his money her way. Frank no longer cared about the money; he grieved for the loss of his dear Rosa.

Carol had just about bled her father dry, when someone showed up on her door step. It was the police. It had been six years since she worked at the accounting firm. She was feeling quite smug; she had done a very good job of covering her tracks. What she couldn't know was that the firm hired someone just a year ago to check over their books. They were surprised to find that a great deal of money had been skimmed off their accounts. It all pointed to Carol. The firm decided to take what they had learned to the police. They were now at her door. The police questioned Carol, but she was able to answer them quite easily. They finally left after two hours of grilling her.

Carol knew it wasn't over, their questions were superficial, and they had been dancing around her, trying to get a feel for the type of person she was. This was her worst nightmare. She thought about what she could do next. One thing for sure, she couldn't stick around here. She was in a tricky spot, and knew she would have to play this game quite carefully.

Later that week, Frank fell down the stairs. In performing his head over heels tumble down the staircase he broke his neck, he could be with his lovely Rosa once again.

The family held a wake for their father. He was always a good man and well loved by those who knew him. Carol, Richard and Vince put together a traditional funeral for their father. There were two full days of wakes followed by the funeral on the third morning. He would be interred next to Rosa, and his story was over.

When Vince got together with Carol and Richard, he found there wasn't much left to the estate. The cash was gone, and all that seemed to remain was the house. When Vince asked Carol about it, she was adamant that the cost of looking after their father was more than they had guessed. Of course she would be glad to show them the records. Carol informed her brothers she no longer wanted to live in that house alone; there were too many memories for her.

The three of them worked together to spruce the house up just enough to be able to sell it quickly. They divided the cash earned from the sale of the house, and went their separate ways once again.

Carol moved away, no one was quite sure where she went. They knew she was gone because the police came by both Richard's and Vince's home to ask if they knew where she was. Of course they didn't; it was Carol's intent to disappear for awhile until the whole mess was forgotten. She disappeared until the statute of limitations for her crime was well past. Then it would be safe to be seen again.

As she took her leave of the state of New Jersey, she wondered if her brothers would ever suspect the truth.

Chapter 7

Vince was happy with his family, and it seemed that everyone was satisfied to be together. What he didn't realize is that nothing stays the same. That sometimes there is nothing you can do to change your fate. And though you may walk away from fate for awhile, she always makes you face the thing that you must do.

What Vince didn't know, is that his wife was having an affair. While he was at work, an old high school sweet heart had drifted into town. Ross had loved Norma years ago, and never got over her. He had gone away to college, but could find no success for himself. One day Ross was trying to decide what to do with himself, and the thought occurred to him that he should return to his roots. Perhaps then he could find a way out of this life he had built for himself. He wasn't happy; and didn't think it was possible for him to be happy.

He came into town, and found Norma. He felt as if his youth had been returned. The vigor, in which he approached Norma, made her soon succumb to Ross's charms.

Norma thought of Ross as a diversion at first; from what she couldn't really say. Life with Vince was good. He never abused her in any way, either verbally or physically. She knew there were relationships out there that had both elements. It would not be a life she would want for herself. So why she decided to have an affair with Ross was unclear even to her.

The affair went on in secret for several months, but this was not a particularly big town. People started to talk, slowly the word spread through town until it was no longer possible for Vince to ignore the signs. He was no longer just looking at nonverbal signs given by Norma; he was hearing stories about his own wife from others in town.

When Vince finally confronted Norma, she broke down and cried. It seemed she had fallen in love with Ross, and was no longer interested in living with Vince. He couldn't understand the whole situation, how could this be? They were happy weren't they? They had such similar likes, and did so many things together. What could have gone so wrong?

It seemed no one had answers for these questions. All anyone knew is that everything had gone terribly wrong for Vince.

Vince moved out into a small apartment in town. He continued at work, still living in the same town with his ex wife while she flaunted her new love about town. This was a very difficult time for Vince. He still loved Norma; he hadn't had the time to adjust to the situation as Norma had.

What made things worse, was that his children would visit him and tell their father stories of abuse. Ross was not kind to Norma. The division of the family had been peaceful. The girls all wanted to continue living together. They would stay with their mother; as she was home all day and visit with their father. It was an adequate arrangement for Vince at the present. He had the ability to see his daughters, and hope for the return of his wife.

Norma was not interested in trying to get back together. Ross was rough, this was true. But there was still something very attractive about him. She found she could even handle the way he treated her. His moods had come upon her gradually, before she knew it she was in a relationship that was not a good situation. She didn't like the hitting, but she couldn't seem to find a way out. So, Norma found ways of dealing with Ross's behavior. She couldn't admit to Vince that she had made a mistake. The town was too small; she didn't feel that Vince could take her back under present circumstances. Norma fell deeper into her chosen path, and could not extricate herself. She was completely dependent on Ross.

Vince was visiting his brother Richard one weekend. He found it so relaxing on the sea shore. While there, Vince was walking along the beach and noticed a cottage for sale. He spoke to Richard about it. Richard was surprised. Cottages were not often available for sale. Richard felt certain he should look into the particulars of the place. Vince needed a place to be that was away from his wife. His daughters could always come to visit. Richard and Vince talked through the situation, and Vince finally saw this as an opportunity to change his life. It was a chance for him to take a look at his life. Introspection was needed. He had dabbled in meditation and spirituality; maybe he needed this time to heal himself. Certainly the time could be well spent to take a view of his life from afar.

Chapter 8

Vince moved his life to the sea. It was exactly what he had needed. Here he could take long walks on the beach. The time spent alone allowed him time to think about the direction of his life. It was certainly a strange life. From the moment of his birth, nothing was quite normal. He thought through the details.

First he was born dead. That had to mean something. Spending the first 30 minutes of your life not breathing, and then as an adult having normal intelligence was a rare thing. The fact that the doctor who brought him into this world disappeared and was untraceable, what could that mean? In some ways that part of his life seemed stranger than the first thirty minutes. No one ever heard of Doctor Scott. He certainly seemed real enough to his parents. This was a deep mystery for Vince. And so he would walk and think. Think about all the people in his life and how he was brought to this place at this time.

Vince's daughters would visit him regularly and as often as they could. Their mother was not really happy on the path she had chosen, but they all knew she was committed to this path, and would not change course.

Vince also took opportunity during his time alone to spend more time with his guitar. He started making new friends in the area. Eventually he found other men of like mind, and they formed a little band. They would get together and play at each others' homes, or on the beach. Once in awhile they would be invited to play at one of the local establishments. He was having fun again and was happy with the new direction of his life.

Vince went deeper into his own spirituality seeking the silence that can reveal the answers to questions asked and unasked. He was becoming stronger in many ways. He thought there was significance to his wife choosing to do the things she had at this time in his life. This is often true for those individuals who have very specific reasons for being here in this life. When it is time for that person to be pulled from their complacency, when it is necessary for them to see beyond the lives they have created for themselves, then it is time for some force to intervene. These forces will uproot your very existence. Either the person digs deep into their soul and develops the tools they require to accomplish their task, or the turmoil stays and eventually that person crumbles from repeated failures.

He knew he needed help, but really had no idea where to start. He thought about going to a psychic, but felt unsure how to proceed. There are some people with true talent in these areas, but how to find one of these individuals? He felt strongly that he must unravel the mystery of his birth. One day, he opened up a bit to one of his friends and told him the details of his birth. This friend was understanding, and thankfully did not laugh when he heard the story. Vince always kept these spiritual things to himself; it was difficult to share these events and feelings with others. He never knew if people would take him seriously. He was baring his soul, and knew he could only do so with a person he felt he could trust implicitly.

Vince was lucky. This person knew of someone whose heritage was with the displaced Cherokee that knew how to get to the root of a problem such as Vince's. He got Vince an appointment to see Paul, the Cherokee descendant.

Paul was an interesting man, and Vince soon felt at ease with him. He told Paul everything. He told him about his birth. He told him about his death. He told Paul about his grandmother Martha. He told him the stories his grandfather had told him about his own mother. He talked about his sister Carol and her strange behavior. Vince even broke down and told Paul that he suspected that his sister Carol had caused his father' demise. He had never shared that thought with anyone, but he knew he could hold nothing back with this man. He felt as if he was on the brink of a great discovery; the discovery of himself.

Paul listened long and carefully.

"Vincent, I understand your concern, and it seems to me that this is about something very big, more than I can handle or discover on my own."

This response shocked Vince. He thought for sure that Paul would tell him something more specific. The fact that he wouldn't or couldn't give him an instant response made him nervous and afraid.

"Vincent, I don't know the answers to all you want to know yet. But, I sometimes work with two other people on difficult cases such as these. Would you be willing to tell your story to the three of us at once?"

Vince agreed, what else could he do? It seemed clear that Paul took him very seriously. There was need for seriousness. When he thought about it, maybe he should have viewed his life with much more seriousness. Look where he was.

It took some time, but Paul did as he promised he arranged a meeting with his three psychic partners. It would be a phone meeting this time. Vince would be with Paul. Another member of the triangle would be calling in from Denver. The third member would call in from Florida.

Paul explained that the triangle was necessary to draw strength from all levels. We are not just physical beings. One person would represent the past. One would represent the present and the third person in the triangle would represent the future. The power of three is strong and represents the birth of true wisdom. There are many examples of the significance of three. Mind, Body and Spirit. The Father, The Son and the Holy Spirit.

"When the three of us work together in this mind set, we can find sense in the variable nature of what has happened to you all your life. We can understand your life in the divine oneness, and bring that knowledge back to you."

"Please tell us everything that comes to your mind. It doesn't matter how small or insignificant it may seem to you, tell us, and hold nothing back, even if you think it may not really apply. Tell us."

"As we listen, we will free ourselves from this physical world, and experience your story in such a way as to bring clarity to what you must do."

So, they listened. When the story was complete to the present, they thanked Vince and told him they would meditate on what they had heard. They would all meet again in two weeks just as they had this day.

In meditation they would escape this world which is not real. The real world lies much closer to the dream world. It is a reality we have all forgotten in the midst of our many mundane tasks. These tasks keep us from our true selves. We stay locked in the mystery of the world our minds created from our wildest dreams. They would now engage in their true being to help Vince understand.

They called on the counsel, upper echelons, angels and higher self to help them and they flew on the path to discovery.

Chapter 9

The three shamans took their time in sorting through the images, words and impressions they received on their inner journey. They discussed what they had learned, until they felt they had put together the entire story. The results were unnerving and dark. It was critical that they relay to Vincent the things they had learned in a gentle way. It would do no good to unnerve him or scare him. Vince had an important task before him, and they knew that it was critical to convince him to own this task and be committed to what he must do.

Paul got in touch with Vince and asked him to be ready to have at least a two hour discussion about the things the shaman had learned. He asked Vince to stay open minded. He advised Vince to look at the story objectively; to accept what he felt in his heart was true. He was further advised to track those things which did not make sense at this time. To write these things down, and see if they would begin to make sense as he traveled on this journey.

"Vince, we are now going to share the story we felt covered all the information we received. Please let us go through our explanation of what we observed before asking questions. Then, we will answer your questions, and help you as much as we can"

About three hundred years ago, there was a man who was very greedy and owned most of the town he lived in. He ran that town with the mindset that he must make more money, his appetite for physical comforts and the money that bought these things was boundless. He owned almost every shop in town, but there was still one business that remained out of his reach. The owner of that business refused to sell to the greedy man at any price. He did not believe it was good for one man to have so much and to have that much power. So, he set his will against the greedy man.

The greedy man devised a plan that would win him the business he so craved. The plan cost the independent business man his life. The greedy man lusted for the wife of the business man, and subsequently desired to marry his widow though the widow resisted. In this way he achieved his goal and had complete control of the town. He only had the opportunity to enjoy his victory for a short time. On a journey to a neighboring town there was an accident, and the man lost his life.

His next move showed us that a great evil existed in this man. And that evil has been at work in your family since that day.

Please listen, that man existed as himself and an evil entity that took control of him. That evil dedicated itself to the destruction of your family as a vengeance for the trouble your ancestor had given him. The evil endured through the centuries by inhabiting the women in your family. As one woman passed on, it would travel to the next likely host. How this entity chose its new human host is unknown. It is important you find a way to understand how the entity chooses its next dwelling place. It is what you were born to do. You must find a way to end this evil now. You are the last male in your family. You are the last protector, the last one that stands between this evil and its ability to grow.

"What about my brother, he could do it?" Vince was beginning to panic.

"No, he doesn't have the strength and knowledge that you do. You and he are the last males, the last ones who can protect against this evil. The strength is not within him. You chose at the moment of your birth to do this task. This is why you were born. It is something only you can do."

The reason you were born dead, was because you were unsure of whether you could take on this burden. It took you thirty minutes to review and finally decide that you would accept this task. Make no mistake; that was no ordinary doctor that was present for your birth. Special Forces and spirit were in place to give you the opportunity to refuse the task. You are here; you accepted this task. We do not know how you will do what must be done, but we know that knowledge is in you. You must give this thought and decide how you will accomplish this task.

We all believe this evil resides in your sister at this point. When your sister dies, this evil will look to go into the next woman in your family. If it succeeds, the results will be disastrous. There will be no protector to stop it.

You must examine this problem. Decide what must be done to stop this evil. We can advise you to think about the next most likely target. You must be prepared to act at the moment of your sister's death. Meditate, consider what path you must take, what actions you must take. You must not fail. You are the only one who can change the path of this great evil. It is your task.

Chapter 10

Vince was floored for days by what the shamans had told him. If his sister were to pass now, he would be held motionless in the spell of the story, and he would fail. He had to absorb all this knowledge, organize it in his mind, make sense of the incredible tale that he knew to be true. It felt right and true to his life. He knew there was a purpose to his life, but he had never imagined that it would be something like this. He felt he couldn't even talk to anyone about his problem.

Vince did finally confide in his brother, but Richard was also at a loss. They talked about possible ways to accomplish the task, but nothing became clear.

Vince took to walking the shore. He found great solace in the endless sounds of the waves hitting the shore. There was a peace here he could not feel anywhere else. He thought about the continuous turn of events that allowed him to be in this space at this time. If things hadn't taken the turn they had, he might never realize his purpose in life. He wondered about the powers that influenced his life so that he could be aware of the responsibilities he had taken on at his birth. Would these powers help him again when it was needed? The answer was that he didn't know. So, he walked the beach thinking, meditating trying to find the answer to this impossible situation.

One day when staring out into the ocean, Vince thought he saw something a few hundred feet off shore. He kept watching trying to put a name to what he saw. The ancient magic of the Earth was at work. He thought he knew what he saw, but the scientist within him was finding it difficult to believe the truth of what he thought he saw. Maybe he was going mad. Maybe the loss of oxygen during his first thirty minutes of life, or death, depending on how you viewed it, was finally taking its toll on him.

He finally turned from the ocean, and saw a set of unusual patterns in the sand. There were thin lines in the sand that looked like they were taking steps from the ocean up onto the beach. He wondered, but felt compelled to follow these lines up the beach. Where the lines ended, he found an unusual pattern set in the sand. In spots, it looked very familiar, as if he should know what it was trying to tell him. He felt certain of one thing; this was a message from the sea. He could barely bring himself to put a name to the writer of the message. He felt if he were to speak it out loud, that he would be deemed certifiably insane.

Vince decided to copy this message on paper and take his time to try and decipher its meaning. The message took his mind off the problem of his life task, but it added another dimension of mystery to his life. He was drawn more to the sea than ever. He looked for things, beings to appear out of the sea. What triggered the appearance of this being out of Earth's magical past?

He found that his life consisted of work, music and the sea. His music gave him a means to relax. His work gave him a chance to think of scientific mysteries. And the sea allowed him to think of the mysteries of this Earth and his life.

It took Vince several weeks, and then he finally realized that the message was written in English. It was not written in a linear fashion, but rather in groups of letter and numbers.

The message read "Did you cry at 911".

He had been hoping secretly for a solution to his life. But it wasn't meant to be. It was true that he had to find the answer within himself.

But why the message about the September eleventh attacks?

He felt compelled to take this message to the three shamans. He felt if he was destined to live in this world of magic and mystery, he should try to understand more about it. This Earth was certainly more than it appeared to be to most of the worlds' population.

This time, the shamans felt the Earth was giving Vince a chance to feel the energy and start to understand the way the energy worked. In their world they knew that this sudden and unexpected loss of life had left many of the souls looking for the light. The light supplies the way to leave the physical form and return to our true selves. Many of the souls who passed on during this incident were seeking light in any form, and were attaching themselves to the light workers of the world. The light workers shone brightly to them, and in their confusion of being ripped from their physical forms, they sought them out. The shamans felt this was a message to Vince to help those people who had attached themselves to him to find the true light out of this physical world. It was a worthy journey for Vince, and gave him some experience within his chosen path.

The shamans worked with Vince giving him some training in this matter. After all, he needed to be free and clear to find the answer to the puzzle of his birth. Vince learned how to send these souls to their true home. It was more preparation for him to accomplish his task. He knew now that anything he observed that would point to the magic and mystery of this world would need to be addressed. It would be further preparation and training and he could not turn from the mystery or instruction. He needed every tool he could develop. And again he knew there were few people he could confide in.

In this world of magic, the people of the Earth forgot their true nature. For the most part people no longer believe in the endless possibilities that exist for this Earth. They have become easy targets by embracing the belief that nothing magical exists. They are not aware of the basic magic within. So, for the most part people scoff and ridicule those that do believe in the possibilities. They exist happily in their cocoons.

Chapter 11

Time passed. Vince learned as much as he could about energy and how it really worked in this world. His sister had become unwell, and he knew that the time of her death would be imminent.

Carol was evil, and he would have nothing to do with her. He did not want to be tainted by her in any way. But, without contact, how would he know when she passed on?

Richard volunteered to keep in touch with her. His job would be to tell Vince the moment she passed on. Vince made sure everyone had cell phones on them. He knew when the time came the communications would have to be instantaneous. There would be little time to act and put an end to this evil.

It wasn't long before the call came. And suddenly Vince knew; he knew exactly what to do to stop this evil from continuing on. Many people experience this instant of knowing exactly what needs to be done for particular instants in time. But, they don't trust their instincts. These moments of knowing come as communications from your guides and masters. They are telling you what to do to achieve the outcome you desire. This time Vince listened, he had been training himself for this moment.

He started calling his daughters. First he called Terry. He felt she was the most likely candidate because of her abilities psychically. Then he called his other daughters. They all received the same message.

"Think only positive thoughts."

"Fill your heart with love"

"No matter what happens do not let any negative or sad thoughts enter your being."

Vince knew that any negative thoughts would give the entity the route into his daughters' soul.

To fight this evil, it was as simple as keeping love and happiness in their thoughts.

But, as simple as it sounds, it is not always an easy thing to do. Furthermore, he knew they would have to keep the warm and loving feelings going for awhile, how long, he wasn't sure of.

Richard worked to bury Carol as quickly as possible. The brothers were anxious to get this over with as soon as possible. They had decided that a wake was not necessary. Carol had made more enemies in her relatively short life than friends. The entity had made sure of that. There would be no need to waste time with a wake when they knew no one would attend except to console her brothers. They needed no consolation. Carol would be interred in less than forty eight hours after her death.

During that time, his daughters needed to keep their spirits high and light hearted. The entity did not make it easy on them. It threw obstacles in their path that would normally be upsetting to say the least. But, they all knew what was at stake. They trusted their father and knew this was necessary. They set their minds to the task, and were determined not to fail their father and themselves in this task.

During the time from Carol's death to the time she was buried, Terry was exposed to physical threat in the form of a car accident. The night Carol died Terry was driving on a country road. A car came along and forced her off the road into a concrete abutment. Her heart was pounding, but the experience was surreal. She knew that under ordinary circumstances she should be feeling intense fear as the car made its way in slow motion toward the concrete abutment. She felt wonder, and in the slowing of time that often goes with a life threatening experience, she knew she had to keep a level of peace in her heart. She needed to infuse love into the situation. First put the feeling of love in her mind and heart, and then let it spread into the situation that was encompassing her. As the scene unfolded she knew she needed to maintain that energy. She needed to keep those good feelings alive in herself. This was necessary in order to keep control over her life. She dug deep within her being and found the strength to pull all those good feelings forward. She was successful. The entity could not find a foothold within her.

The entity tried similar, if not such drastic methods with the other girls. It knew that Terry was strong in the magic of this Earth. It had set circumstances in motion to cause the car accident for Terry, and was sure the accident would give the desired effect, but it didn't. She was too strong. Well, there were the other three girls.

Try as it might to create circumstances that would start them down a path of negativity, the entity could not succeed. Vince had done too good a job of tutoring his daughters in what they needed to do. They kept control of themselves, because not one of them wanted to end up like their aunt Carol.

Richard and Vince attended the funeral; he would not allow his daughters to attend. He knew that the entity would be there looking for a way to move to its next victim. Preying on emotional negativity was the way it had operated throughout history. Vince was on the lookout for any sign of the entity.

The funeral went smoothly. Carol's body was taken directly to the church. It was early March, and there had been a freak ice storm that night. The brothers were determined to have Carol buried that day. They could not afford a delay. So, Carol's body was taken to the church over slush covered streets. It was a beautiful pristine day. The sky was clear, the air was crisp. The trees were covered wIth ice and were sparkling in the sunshine.

The funeral director had the body brought into the small brick country church. Richard and Vince were pall bearers, but, the funeral home had to supply the remaining pall bearers to get her body into the church.

The priest began attending to the body. A full mass was not performed. The priest covered the casket in traditional church vestments. The Paschal candle was lit, as it is when sacraments are performed. In this case the priest performed the sacrament of Extreme Unction, the anointing of the sick or dead. This is a very effective sacrament, but the sad thing is that this sacrament is often given too late to help. It should be used more freely on the ill.

As the priest was sprinkling holy water on the casket, the water hissed off the surface, rising off in steam. He continued sprinkling the holy water, and it continued to steam off the casket. Then with a finality that could not be conveyed in words, the ice covered branches outside the church started breaking and crashing on the roof. The priest stood back, unsure what to think. When the ceremony was complete, the casket was taken out back to be buried in the church cemetery.

When the ceremony was complete, the priest went off on his own, wandering in the churchyard, thinking about the events that had just transpired. Richard noticed him, and decided to approach the priest that had put the seal on Carol's coffin. He walked up to the priest and just looked pleadingly in his eyes:

"Father?"

"Don't worry, it's over"

Vince followed his brother to the priest. The three of them talked about Carol and the unusual events of her funeral. They wrapped and infused the entity with love putting an end to its hunger. They all walked away feeling satisfied that the task was done. The entity had been contained.

EPILOG

Vince often walked by the shore reflecting on his life's work so far. Feeling he had accomplished the major goal of his life, but wishing for confirmation.

Vince walked and wondered about all the things that had transpired in his life. He had been guided along the path, and given all the tools he needed to succeed. He knew that guidance would always be there. He was thankful that he had become aware of this guidance, and could appreciate it for what it was. He had received guidance from beyond the limits of this world to fix an ancient evil.

As he walked the shoreline, he noticed something out in the ocean. Could it be? Was she waiting to give him another message? Was it possible that he could be seeing her again? He still was having trouble believing that he had ever seen her in the first place. Clearly the magic of the Earth was active again.

Vince felt something nudging at his foot. He was reluctant to turn from the sea. He had hoped he would get a better look this time. The nudge was relentless, and he knew he must look from the sea to what he felt against his foot. There was a stone hitting the side of his foot. He felt compelled to pick it up and really look at it.

He did receive another message from the sea. On the stone was an image engraved upon it. The image was that of a child being strangled by his own umbilical cord.

The mystery of his birth was returned to him from the sea, confirming his success.